I0654860

James Russell Lowell

Last Poems

James Russell Lowell

Last Poems

ISBN/EAN: 9783744770200

Printed in Europe, USA, Canada, Australia, Japan

Cover: Foto ©Andreas Hilbeck / pixelio.de

More available books at **www.hansebooks.com**

Etched from a photograph taken at Whitby England in 1889
Æt. 70

LAST POEMS

OF

JAMES RUSSELL LOWELL

BOSTON AND NEW YORK
HOUGHTON, MIFFLIN AND COMPANY
The Riverside Press, Cambridge
M DCCC XCV

Copyright, 1895,
By CHARLES ELIOT NORTON.

All rights reserved.

Electrotyped and Printed by H. O. Houghton & Co.
The Riverside Press, Cambridge, Mass., U. S. A.

THIS little volume contains those of the poems which Mr. Lowell wrote in his last years which, I believe, he might have wished to preserve. Three of them were published before his death. Of the rest, two appear here for the first time.

C. E. N.

September, 1895.

CONTENTS

LAST POEMS

HOW I CONSULTED THE ORA-CLE OF THE GOLDFISHES

WHAT know we of the world im-
mense
Beyond the narrow ring of sense?
What should we know, who lounge about
The house we dwell in, nor find out,
Masked by a wall, the secret cell
Where the soul's priests in hiding dwell?
The winding stair that steals aloof
To chapel-mysteries 'neath the roof?

It lies about us, yet as far
From sense sequestered as a star
New launched its wake of fire to trace
In secrecies of unprobed space,
Whose beacon's lightning-pinioned spears

Might earthward haste a thousand years
Nor reach it. So remote seems this
World undiscovered, yet it is
A neighbor near and dumb as death,
So near, we seem to feel the breath
Of its hushed habitants as they
Pass us unchallenged, night and day.

Never could mortal ear nor eye
By sound or sign suspect them nigh,
Yet why may not some subtler sense
Than those poor two give evidence ?
Transfuse the ferment of their being
Into our own, past hearing, seeing,
As men, if once attempered so,
Far off each other's thought can know ?
As horses with an instant thrill
Measure their rider's strength of will ?
Comes not to all some glimpse that brings
Strange sense of sense-escaping things ?
Wraiths some transfigured nerve divines ?

8

Approaches, premonitions, signs,
Voices of Ariel that die out
In the dim No Man's Land of Doubt?

Are these Night's dusky birds? Are these
Phantasmas of the silences
Outer or inner? — rude heirlooms
From grovellers in the cavern-glooms,
Who in unhuman Nature saw
Misshapen foes with tusk and claw,
And with those night-fears brute and blind
Peopled the chaos of their mind,
Which, in ungovernable hours,
Still make their bestial lair in ours?

Were they, or were they not? Yes; no;
Uncalled they come, unbid they go,
And leave us fumbling in a doubt
Whether within us or without
The spell of this illusion be
That witches us to hear and see

9

As in a twi-life what it will,
And hath such wonder-working skill
That what we deemed most solid-wrought
Turns a mere figment of our thought,
Which when we grasp at in despair
Our fingers find vain semblance there,
For Psyche seeks a corner-stone
Firmer than aught to matter known.

Is it illusion ?   Dream-stuff ?   Show
Made of the wish to have it so ?
'T were something, even though this were
       all :
So the poor prisoner, on his wall
Long gazing, from the chance designs
Of crack, mould, weather-stain, refines
New and new pictures without cease,
Landscape, or saint, or altar-piece :
But these are Fancy's common brood
Hatched in the nest of solitude ;
This is Dame Wish's hourly trade,

By our rude sires a goddess made.
Could longing, though its heart broke,
    give
Trances in which we chiefly live?
Moments that darken all beside,
Tearfully radiant as a bride?
Beckonings of bright escape, of wings
Purchased with loss of baser things?
Blithe truancies from all control
Of Hylë, outings of the soul?

The worm, by trustful instinct led,
Draws from its womb a slender thread,
And drops, confiding that the breeze
Will waft it to unpastured trees:
So the brain spins itself, and so
Swings boldly off in hope to blow
Across some tree of knowledge, fair
With fruitage new, none else shall share:
Sated with wavering in the Void,
It backward climbs, so best employed,

And, where no proof is nor can be,
Seeks refuge with Analogy;
Truth's soft half-sister, she may tell
Where lurks, seld-sought, the other's
    well.
With metaphysic midges sore,
My Thought seeks comfort at her door,
And, at her feet a suppliant cast,
Evokes a spectre of the past.
Not such as shook the knees of Saul,
But winsome, golden-gay withal, —
Two fishes in a globe of glass,
That pass, and waver, and re-pass,
And lighten that way, and then this,
Silent as meditation is.
With a half-humorous smile I see
In this their aimless industry,
These errands nowhere and returns
Grave as a pair of funeral urns,
This ever-seek and never-find,
A mocking image of my mind.

But not for this I bade you climb
Up from the darkening deeps of time :
Help me to tame these wild day-mares
That sudden on me unawares.
Fish, do your duty, as did they
Of the Black Island far away
In life's safe places, — far as you
From all that now I see or do.
You come, embodied flames, as when
I knew you first, nor yet knew men ;
Your gold renews my golden days,
Your splendor all my loss repays.

'T is more than sixty years ago
Since first I watched your to-and-fro ;
Two generations come and gone
From silence to oblivion,
With all their noisy strife and stress
Lulled in the grave's forgivingness,
While you unquenchably survive
Immortal, almost more alive.

I watched you then a curious boy,
Who in your beauty found full joy,
And, by no problem-debts distrest,
Sate at life's board a welcome guest.
You were my sister's pets, not mine ;
But Property's dividing line
No hint of dispossession drew
On any map my simplesse knew ;
O golden age, not yet dethroned !
What made me happy, that I owned ;
You were my wonders, you my Lars,
In darkling days my sun and stars,
And over you entranced I hung,
Too young to know that I was young.
Gazing with still unsated bliss,
My fancies took some shape like this :
" I have my world, and so have you,
A tiny universe for two,
A bubble by the artist blown,
Scarcely more fragile than our own,
Where you have all a whale could wish,

Happy as Eden's primal fish.
Manna is dropt you thrice a day
From some kind heaven not far away,
And still you snatch its softening crumbs,
Nor, more than we, think whence it comes.
No toil seems yours but to explore
Your cloistered realm from shore to shore ;
Sometimes you trace its limits round,
Sometimes its limpid depths you sound,
Or hover motionless midway,
Like gold-red clouds at set of day ;
Erelong you whirl with sudden whim
Off to your globe's most distant rim,
Where, greatened by the watery lens,
Methinks no dragon of the fens
Flashed huger scales against the sky,
Roused by Sir Bevis or Sir Guy,
And the one eye that meets my view,
Lidless and strangely largening, too,
Like that of conscience in the dark,
Seems to make me its single mark.

What a benignant lot is yours
That have an own All-out-of-doors,
No words to spell, no sums to do,
No Nepos and no parlyvoo!
How happy you without a thought
Of such cross things as Must and Ought, —
I too the happiest of boys
To see and share your golden joys!"

So thought the child, in simpler words,
Of you his finny flocks and herds;
Now, an old man, I bid you rise
To the fine sight behind the eyes,
And, lo, you float and flash again
In the dark cistern of my brain.
But o'er your visioned flames I brood
With other mien, in other mood;
You are no longer there to please,
But to stir argument, and tease
My thought with all the ghostly shapes
From which no moody man escapes.

16

Diminished creature, I no more
Find Fairyland beside my door,
But for each moment's pleasure pay
With the *quart d'heure* of Rabelais !

I watch you in your crystal sphere,
And wonder if you see and hear
Those shapes and sounds that stir the wide
Conjecture of a world outside ;
In your pent lives, as we in ours,
Have you surmises dim of powers,
Of presences obscurely shown,
Of lives a riddle to your own,
Just on the senses' outer verge,
Where sense-nerves into soul-nerves merge,
Where we conspire our own deceit
Confederate in deft Fancy's feat,
And the fooled brain befools the eyes
With pageants woven of its own lies ?
But *are* they lies ? Why more than those
Phantoms that startle your repose,

Half seen, half heard, then flit away,
And leave you your prose-bounded day?

The things ye see as shadows I
Know to be substance; tell me why
My visions, like those haunting you,
May not be as substantial too.
Alas, who ever answer heard
From fish, and dream-fish too? Absurd!
Your consciousness I half divine,
But you are wholly deaf to mine.
Go, I dismiss you; ye have done
All that ye could; our silk is spun:
Dive back into the deep of dreams,
Where what is real is what seems!
Yet I shall fancy till my grave
Your lives to mine a lesson gave;
If lesson none, an image, then,
Impeaching self-conceit in men
Who put their confidence alone
In what they call the Seen and Known.

How seen ? How known ? As through
    your glass
Our wavering apparitions pass
Perplexingly, then subtly wrought
To some quite other thing by thought.
Here shall my resolution be :
The shadow of the mystery
Is haply wholesomer for eyes
That cheat us to be overwise,
And I am happy in my right
To love God's darkness as His light.

   10th May, 1889.

TURNER'S OLD TÉMÉRAIRE

UNDER A FIGURE SYMBOLIZING THE CHURCH

THOU wast the fairest of all man-
    made things ;
The breath of heaven bore up thy cloudy
    wings,
And, patient in their triple rank,
The thunders crouched about thy flank,
Their black lips silent with the doom of
    kings.

The storm-wind loved to rock him in thy
    pines,
And swell thy vans with breath of great
    designs ;
Long-wildered pilgrims of the main
By thee relaid their course again,
Whose prow was guided by celestial signs.

20

How didst thou trample on tumultuous
seas,
Or, like some basking sea-beast stretched
at ease,
Let the bull-fronted surges glide
Caressingly along thy side,
Like glad hounds leaping by the hunts-
man's knees !

Heroic feet, with fire of genius shod,
In battle's ecstasy thy deck have trod,
While from their touch a fulgor ran
Through plank and spar, from man to man,
Welding thee to a thunderbolt of God.

Now a black demon, belching fire and
steam,
Drags thee away, a pale, dismantled dream,
And all thy desecrated bulk
Must landlocked lie, a helpless hulk,
To gather weeds in the regardless stream.

Woe 's me, from Ocean's sky-horizoned
    air
To this! Better, the flame-cross still
    aflare,
Shot-shattered to have met thy doom
Where thy last lightnings cheered the
    gloom,
Than here be safe in dangerless despair.

Thy drooping symbol to the flagstaff
    clings,
Thy rudder soothes the tide to lazy rings,
Thy thunders now but birthdays greet,
Thy planks forget the martyrs' feet,
Thy masts what challenges the sea-wind
    brings.

Thou a mere hospital, where human
    wrecks,
Like winter-flies, crawl those renownèd
    decks,

Ne'er trodden save by captive foes,
And wonted sternly to impose
God's will and thine on bowed imperial
    necks !

Shall nevermore, engendered of thy fame,
A new sea-eagle heir thy conqueror name,
And with commissioned talons wrench
From thy supplanter's grimy clench
His sheath of steel, his wings of smoke
    and flame ?

This shall the pleased eyes of our chil-
    dren see ;
For this the stars of God long even as we ;
Earth listens for his wings ; the Fates
Expectant lean ; Faith cross-propt waits,
And the tired waves of Thought's insur-
    gent sea.

1888.

ST. MICHAEL THE WEIGHER

S TOOD the tall Archangel weighing
All man's dreaming, doing, saying,
All the failure and the pain,
All the triumph and the gain,
In the unimagined years,
Full of hopes, more full of tears,
Since old Adam's hopeless eyes
Backward searched for Paradise,
And, instead, the flame-blade saw
Of inexorable Law.

Waking, I beheld him there,
With his fire-gold, flickering hair,
In his blinding armor stand,
And the scales were in his hand :
Mighty were they, and full well

24

They could poise both heaven and hell.
" Angel," asked I humbly then,
" Weighest thou the souls of men?
That thine office is, I know."
" Nay," he answered me, " not so :
But I weigh the hope of Man
Since the power of choice began,
In the world, of good or ill."
Then I waited and was still.

In one scale I saw him place
All the glories of our race,
Cups that lit Belshazzar's feast,
Gems, the lightning of the East,
Kublai's sceptre, Cæsar's sword,
Many a poet's golden word,
Many a skill of science, vain
To make men as gods again.

In the other scale he threw
Things regardless, outcast, few,

Martyr-ash, arena sand,
Of St. Francis' cord a strand,
Beechen cups of men whose need
Fasted that the poor might feed,
Disillusions and despairs
Of young saints with grief-grayed hairs,
Broken hearts that brake for Man.

Marvel through my pulses ran
Seeing then the beam divine
Swiftly on this hand decline,
While Earth's splendor and renown
Mounted light as thistle-down.

1888.

A VALENTINE

LET others wonder what fair face
    Upon their path shall shine,
And, fancying half, half hoping, trace
    Some maiden shape of tenderest grace
        To be their Valentine.

Let other hearts with tremor sweet
    One secret wish enshrine
That Fate may lead their happy feet
    Fair Julia in the lane to meet
        To be their Valentine.

But I, far happier, am secure ;
    I know the eyes benign,
The face more beautiful and pure
    Than Fancy's fairest portraiture
        That mark my Valentine.

27

More than when first I singled thee,
This only prayer is mine, —
That, in the years I yet shall see,
As, darling, in the past, thou 'lt be
My happy Valentine.

28

ON this wild waste, where never blos-
    som came,
  Save the white wind-flower in the bil-
    low's cap,
Or those pale disks of momentary flame,
  Loose petals dropped from Dian's care-
    less lap,
    What far-fetched influence all my
    fancy fills
    With singing birds and dancing daffo-
    dils?

Why, 't is her day whom jocund April
  brought,

And who brings April with her in her
  eyes ;
It is her vision lights my lonely thought,
  Even as a rose that opes its hushed sur-
    prise
    In sick men's chambers, with its
      glowing breath
    Plants Summer at the glacier edge of
      Death.

Gray sky, sea gray as mossy stones on
  graves ; —
Anon comes April in her jollity ;
And dancing down the bleak vales 'tween
  the waves,
  Makes them green glades for all her
    flowers and me.
    The gulls turn thrushes, charmed are
      sea and sky
    By magic of my thought, and know
      not why.

Ah, but I know, for never April's shine,
  Nor passion gust of rain, nor all her
    flowers
Scattered in haste, were seen so sudden
    fine
  As she in various mood, on whom the
    powers
    Of happiest stars in fair conjunction
    smiled
    To bless the birth of April's darling
    child.

31

LOVE AND THOUGHT

WHAT hath Love with Thought to
do ?
Still at variance are the two.
Love is sudden, Love is rash,
Love is like the levin flash,
Comes as swift, as swiftly goes,
And his mark as surely knows.

Thought is lumpish, Thought is slow,
Weighing long 'tween yes and no ;
When dear Love is dead and gone,
Thought comes creeping in anon,
And, in his deserted nest,
Sits to hold the crowner's quest.

Since we love, what need to think ?
Happiness stands on a brink

Whence too easy 't is to fall
Whither 's no return at all ;
Have a care, half-hearted lover,
Thought would only push her over !

THE NOBLER LOVER

IF he be a nobler lover, take him!
  You in you I seek, and not myself;
Love with men 's what women choose to
    make him,
  Seraph strong to soar, or fawn-eyed elf:
All I am or can, your beauty gave it,
  Lifting me a moment nigh to you,
And my bit of heaven, I fain would save
    it —
  Mine I thought it was, I never knew.

What you take of me is yours to serve
    you,
  All I give, you gave to me before;
Let him win you! If I but deserve you,
  I keep all you grant to him and more:

34

You shall make me dare what others dare
  not,
  You shall keep my nature pure as snow,
And a light from you that others share
  not
Shall transfigure me where'er I go.

Let me be your thrall !   However lowly
  Be the bondsman's service I can do,
Loyalty shall make it high and holy ;
  Naught can be unworthy, done for you.
Men shall say, " A lover of this fashion
  Such an icy mistress well beseems."
Women say, " Could we deserve such pas-
  sion,
We might be the marvel that he dreams."

35

ON HEARING A SONATA OF BEETHOVEN'S PLAYED IN THE NEXT ROOM

UNSEEN Musician, thou art sure to
please,
For those same notes in happier days I
heard
Poured by dear hands that long have
never stirred
Yet now again for me delight the keys:
Ah me, to strong illusions such as these
What are Life's solid things? The
walls that gird
Our senses, lo, a casual scent or word
Levels, and 't is the soul that hears and
sees!
Play on, dear girl, and many be the years

36

Ere some grayhaired survivor sit like
  me
And, for thy largess pay a meed of tears
  Unto another who, beyond the sea
    Of Time and Change, perhaps not
    sadly hears
    A music in this verse undreamed by
    thee !

CHRISTMAS, 1885.

VERSES

IN good old times, which means, you
      know,
The time men wasted long ago,
And we must blame our brains or mood
If that we squander seems less good,
In those blest days when wish was act
And fancy dreamed itself to fact,
Godfathers used to fill with guineas
The cups they gave their pickaninnies,
Performing functions at the chrism
Not mentioned in the Catechism.
No millioner, poor I fill up
With wishes my more modest cup,
Though had I Amalthea's horn

It should be hers the newly born.
Nay, shudder not ! I should bestow it
So brimming full she could n't blow it.
Wishes are n't horses : true, but still
There are worse roadsters than goodwill.
And so I wish my darling health,
And just to round my couplet, wealth,
With faith enough to bridge the chasm
'Twixt Genesis and Protoplasm,
And bear her o'er life's current vext
From this world to a better next,
Where the full glow of God puts out
Poor reason's farthing candle, Doubt.
I 've wished her healthy, wealthy, wise,
But since there 's room for countless wishes
In these old-fashioned posset dishes,
I 'll wish her from my plenteous store
Of those commodities two more,
Her father's wit, veined through and
      through
With tenderness that Watts (but whew !

39

Celia 's aflame, I mean no stricture
On his Sir Josh-surpassing picture)
I wish her next, and 't is the soul
Of all I 've dropt into the bowl,
Her mother's beauty — nay, but two
So fair at once would never do.
Then let her but the half possess,
Troy was besieged ten years for less.
Now if there 's any truth in Darwin,
And we from what was, all we are win,
I simply wish the child to be
A sample of Heredity,
Enjoying to the full extent
Life's best, the Unearned Increment
Which Fate her Godfather to flout
Gave *him* in legacies of gout.
Thus, then, the cup is duly filled ;
Walk steady, dear, lest all be spilled.

ON A BUST OF GENERAL GRANT

STRONG, simple, silent are the [stead-
      fast] laws
That sway this universe, of none withstood,
Unconscious of man's outcries or applause,
Or what man deems his evil or his good ;
And when the Fates ally them with a cause
That wallows in the sea-trough and seems
      lost,
Drifting in danger of the reefs and sands
Of shallow counsels, this way, that way,
      tost,
Strength, silence, simpleness, of these
      three strands
They twist the cable shall the world hold
      fast

To where its anchors clutch the bed-rock
    of the Past.

Strong, simple, silent, therefore such was
    he
Who helped us in our need; the eternal
    law
That who can saddle Opportunity
Is God's elect, though many a mortal flaw
May minish him in eyes that closely see,
Was verified in him : what need we say
Of one who made success where others '
    failed,
Who, with no light save that of common
    day,
Struck hard, and still struck on till Fortune
    quailed,
But that (so sift the Norns) a desperate
    van
Ne'er fell at last to one who was not wholly
    man.

A face all prose where Time's [benignant]
    haze
Softens no raw edge yet, nor makes all
    fair
With the beguiling light of vanished days ;
This is relentless granite, bleak and bare,
Roughhewn, and scornful of æsthetic
    phrase ;
Nothing is here for fancy, naught for
    dreams,
The Present's hard uncompromising light
Accents all vulgar outlines, flaws, and
    seams,
Yet vindicates some pristine natural right
O'ertopping that hereditary grace
Which marks the gain or loss of some
    time-fondled race.

So Marius looked, methinks, and Crom-
    well so,
Not in the purple born, to those they led

Nearer for that and costlier to the foe,

New moulders of old forms, by nature
bred

The exhaustless life of manhood's seeds
to show,

Let but the ploughshare of portentous
times

Strike deep enough to reach them where
they lie :

Despair and danger are their fostering
climes,

And their best sun bursts from a stormy
sky :

He was our man of men, nor would abate

The utmost due manhood could claim of
fate.

Nothing ideal, a plain-people's man

At the first glance, a more deliberate ken

Finds type primeval, theirs in whose veins
ran

Such blood as quelled the dragon in his
    den,
Made harmless fields, and better worlds
    began :
He came grim-silent, saw and did the deed
That was to do ; in his master-grip
Our sword flashed joy ; no skill of words
    could breed
Such sure conviction as that close-clamped
    lip ;
He slew our dragon, nor, so seemed it,
    knew
He had done more than any simplest man
    might do.

Yet did this man, war-tempered, stern as
    steel
Where steel opposed, prove soft in civil
    sway ;
The hand hilt-hardened had lost tact to
    feel

The world's base coin, and glozing knaves
    made prey
Of him and of the entrusted Commonweal;
So Truth insists and will not be denied.
We turn our eyes away, and so will Fame,
As if in his last battle he had died
Victor for us and spotless of all blame,
Doer of hopeless tasks which praters shirk,
One of those still plain men that do the
    world's rough work.

NOTE. — This poem is the last, so far as is known, written by Mr. Lowell. He laid it aside for revision, leaving two of the verses incomplete.

In a pencilled fragment of the poem the first verse appears as follows : —

    " Strong, simple, silent, such are Nature's Laws."

In the final copy, from which the poem is now printed, the verse originally stood : —

    " Strong, steadfast, silent are the   laws,"
but " steadfast " is crossed out, and " simple " written above.

A similar change is made in the ninth verse of the stanza, where "simpleness" is substituted for "steadfastness."

The change from "steadfast" to "simple" was not made, probably through oversight, in the first verse of the second stanza.

There is nothing to indicate what epithet Mr. Lowell would have chosen to complete the first verse of the third stanza.

C. E. N.

www.ingramcontent.com/pod-product-compliance
Lightning Source LLC
Chambersburg PA
CBHW022014050726
47499CB00007BA/2613